This book belongs to

To my husband, Jan,
who showed me Vienna and so much more...
—L.R.L.

For Peter and Jacqui Poole and all your grandchildren
—Love from Alison

THIS IS A BORZOI BOOK PUBLISHED BY ALFRED A. KNOPF

Text copyright © 2014 by Linda Ravin Lodding
Jacket art and interior illustrations copyright © 2014 by Alison Jay

All rights reserved. Published in the United States by Alfred A. Knopf, an imprint of
Random House Children's Books, a division of Random House, Inc., New York.
Originally published in slightly different form in Great Britain by Gullane Children's Books, London, in 2014.

Knopf, Borzoi Books, and the colophon are registered trademarks of Random House, Inc.

Visit us on the Web! randomhouse.com/kids

Educators and librarians, for a variety of teaching tools, visit us at RHTeachersLibrarians.com

Library of Congress Cataloging-in-Publication Data is available upon request.
ISBN 978-0-385-75331-9 (trade)
ISBN 978-0-385-75332-6 (lib. bdg.)

The illustrations in this book were created using alkyd paint and crackle varnish on thick cartridge paper.

MANUFACTURED IN CHINA
March 2014
10 9 8 7 6 5 4 3 2 1
First American Edition

A Gift for Mama

by Linda Ravin Lodding • illustrated by Alison Jay

ALFRED A. KNOPF  NEW YORK

Morning bells rang out over Vienna.
Shoppers and sellers filled the streets, and
carriages clippity-clopped against the cobblestones.
Oskar peered wide-eyed into the shop windows.

It was his mother's birthday, and he wanted
to give her the perfect gift.

The windows were full of treasures.
Cakes, hats, music boxes . . .
What can I buy?
wondered Oskar.

He had only a single coin.

But there, in the middle of the
market, was a flower seller.
A beautiful yellow rose peeked out
from within her basket of blooms.

GRABEN

Schloss

Augarten

The perfect present, thought Oskar, and held out his coin.

As Oskar admired his gift, an artist passed by.
"What a wonderful rose!" he exclaimed.
"How perfect it would be
in the portrait I'm painting!"

"But it's a present for my mama,"
explained Oskar.

"I'll trade you," said the artist. "What do you say—
a beautiful horsehair paintbrush for that beautiful rose?"

Oskar hesitated. . . .

But then he said,

"Of course!
I can paint a picture for Mama—
the perfect present!"

Oskar skipped toward home.

As he passed the Opera House,
he could hear the orchestra rehearsing.
He waved his paintbrush in time with the music.

Just then, a man came running toward him.
"I can't find my conductor's baton!" he cried. "Oh, what will I do?"

Suddenly the conductor beamed with delight.
"*You* have a baton!" he exclaimed.
"Sir, you are mistaken," said Oskar.
"This is a paintbrush."

"Paintbrush, baton, no matter. It can lead an orchestra!"

The conductor held up
a sheet of music.
"I'll trade you!
Here's a melody
I wrote just this morning.

Da Da Da Dee Dum,"
he sang.
"Da Da Da Dee Dum."

"Mama loves music!" said Oskar.
"That's the perfect present."

"Da Da Da Dee Dum,
Dee Dee, Dum Dum . . ."
sang Oskar as he waltzed
down the street.

"Da Da Da Dee Dum,"
Dee Dee, Dum Dum . . . /
another voice joined in.

"That tune," said the man.
"I have the perfect words for it! May I?"
He plucked the music from
Oskar's hand and started to write.

"But that's Mama's birthday song!"
Oskar cried.

"Now I have no present!"

The man rummaged through his satchel.
"Does your mama like books?"
he asked.
"I wrote this one myself."

"Mama loves books,"
said Oskar.

"A book is the perfect present!"

Just then, a commotion
broke out on the street.
Oskar tugged on a lady's sleeve.
"What's happening?" he asked.
"It's the Empress!" she said.
"Her coach is stuck in the mud!"

As Oskar squeezed through the crowd . . .

. . . suddenly a coachman grabbed his book!
He jammed it under the wheel. "Make way!" he shouted.

With a tug on the reins, the carriage lurched to a roll.
"Mama's book!" cried Oskar. "It's ruined."

But as Oskar looked up, there was the Empress herself!
She held out a box. "Candied violets," she said kindly. "To say sorry for your book."

Oskar bowed. "Thank you, Your Highness!"
The dainty, delicious sweets were the perfect gift for Mama!

Oskar ran along the banks of the river Danube.
He couldn't wait to see Mama's face. . . .

But there, on the water's edge,
a girl caught his eye. Even
though her face was covered in tears,
she was the prettiest girl he had ever seen.

"Why are you crying?" asked Oskar.
"Today is my mama's birthday," said the girl.
"An artist was painting my portrait for her.
But he couldn't finish it in time—"

"And now you have no present?" Oskar guessed.
The girl nodded and wiped away a tear.

Oskar held tightly to his box of sweets.

Then, ever so slowly, his fingers loosened.
"Here," he said gently, "give your mama these."

The girl's smile was as sweet as the scent
of the yellow rose pinned to her dress.
"The perfect present!" she said.

Oskar turned toward home.
Dusk was falling, and he knew
Mama would be worried.
He blinked back tears. . . .

What would he
give Mama now?

But suddenly there was
a tap on his shoulder.

"For you," said the girl.
And she handed him
the beautiful yellow rose.

Oskar's heart soared!
Clutching his gift,
he raced through the
darkening streets toward home.

Mama was waiting on the doorstep.
"Happy birthday!" cried Oskar.

Mama smelled the rose.
She wrapped her son in her arms.
"Perfect," she said.

A Note from the Author

In 1994, when I moved to Vienna, I would walk the
cobblestone streets of the "old town" and imagine what this city must
have been like at the turn of the last century. It wasn't hard to picture:
Vienna in 1994 didn't look much different from Vienna in 1894. As I strolled
under the arches of the Hofburg Palace, passed the Opera House and
lingered in front of Demel's coffeehouse—eyeing their candied violets!—
a story came to me. I imagined a boy, Oskar, darting through the old town,
encountering the famous nineteenth-century artists, musicians,
writers and nobility. Everywhere I walked with Oskar, I could
see their shadows in this city—the artist Gustav Klimt,
the musician and composer Johann Strauss II,
the author Felix Salten and the beautiful Empress Sisi.
While *A Gift for Mama* is Oskar's story, this is also
Vienna's story. And now it's yours, too.

Linda Ravin Lodding

For my granddaughter Rachel
P. L.
For Paul, with love
T. M.

Text copyright © 1994 by Penelope Lively
Illustrations copyright © 1994 by Terry Milne

First U.S. edition 1994
Published in Great Britain in 1994
by Walker Books Ltd., London.

Library of Congress Cataloging-in-Publication Data

Lively, Penelope, 1933–
The cat, the crow, and the banyan tree /
Penelope Lively; illustrated by Terry Milne.—
1st U.S. ed.
Summary: A cat and a crow have their own individual
styles of telling stories and one day these styles are displayed
as the two share an exciting adventure.
ISBN 1-56402-325-7
[1. Storytelling—Fiction.   2. Cats—Fiction.   3. Crows—Fiction.]
I. Milne, Terry, 1964– ill. II. Title.
PZ7.L7397Cat   1994
[E]—dc20   93-22355

10 9 8 7 6 5 4 3 2 1

Printed in Italy

The pictures for this book were done in colored ink
on specially treated paper.

Candlewick Press
2067 Massachusetts Avenue
Cambridge, Massachusetts 02140

The Cat, the Crow, and the Banyan Tree

by PENELOPE LIVELY   illustrated by TERRY MILNE

CANDLEWICK PRESS
CAMBRIDGE, MASSACHUSETTS

The cat and the crow lived under the banyan tree.
All day long they told stories.
The cat was thin and quick, and she told stories
that were elegant and entertaining.

The crow was fat and handsome, and he
told stories that were fast and furious.
The banyan tree was tall and wide and
light and dark and full of secrets.

One day the cat said, "Today we're going to tell extra special stories. My turn first. Are you listening, Crow?"
"I'm listening," said the crow.

"Then I'll begin," said the cat. "There was once a crow, and a very fine fellow was he."

"I like this story," said the crow. "Go on."

And then his friend the cat, who was thin and quick and knew mysterious things, told the crow to follow her into the story and at once they found themselves in one of the hidden places of the banyan tree.

"What's this?" said the crow.
"The secret stairs," said the cat.
"Where do they go?" asked the crow.
"On and on and up and up and
around and around and into the
clouds and out the other side."
And the cat told the crow
to follow her up the
stairs, up and up
and on and on.

"I'm getting tired," the crow complained. "A hundred and one, a hundred and two, a hundred and three . . . "

"Here we are!" said the cat. "Look!"
And the crow looked and saw the sky and the stars and the huge bright moon.

"Now what?" said the crow.

"Do you see the mountains of the moon?" asked the cat. "That's where we're going."

"Why?" said the crow.

"To find the end of the story," said the cat.

She called for a shooting star, and the
star pulled them through the clouds and
up into the dark sky, up and up to the
top of the highest mountain on the moon.

The crow looked around.
"So where's the end of the story?"
"Right here," said the cat. "We're at the end of the
story because we climbed the stairs and found the
sky and rode with the star and got to the top of the
highest mountain and now we can see back to the
beginning. Take the telescope and look down."
The crow looked, and
far, far away he saw
the banyan tree.
"There's the
beginning
of the story,"
said the cat.
"Now shut
your eyes and
we'll go back."

When the crow
opened his eyes,
he found that
they were back
underneath the
banyan tree.
"Well," said the
crow. "My turn
now. Quick!
The story's
already begun.
We're off!"
"Where to?" said the cat.
"Anywhere! Everywhere!
Look out! They're after us!"

"Who?" cried the cat.
"Everyone! Anyone!"
"Why?" gasped the cat.

"They're after our money!
Our jewels! Our gold and silver!"
"What gold? What silver?"
"It's the hullabaloos!" yelled the crow.
"Hang on tight—we'll go supersonic!"

"Ooooooh . . ." moaned the cat.
"We've escaped," said the crow. "Help!
Here comes the glockenspiel!"
"I don't like this story,"
wailed the cat.
"I want to
get off."

"It all works out in the
end," said the crow.
"Just you wait. Whoops!
There he goes!
Now for the ghost
tunnel. Keep your
head down and sing."

"Why do
we have to
go in here?"
mewed the cat.
"To get to the other
end," said the crow.
"Sing louder!
Scare them
off! That's
the way! . . .

. . . Out we come!"

"Oooooh . . . " cried the cat.

"Are we almost there?"

"Almost where?" said the
crow. "Look out! Here
comes the snake gang!
Watch your tail! Hold on tight . . .
Wheee! There we go.
Isn't this story fun?"

"I'm not sure," said the cat.

"Where's the end?"

"I think I can see it,"
said the crow. "Pass
me the telescope.
Now—going
supersonic again.
Whoosh . . . "

And there
they were
back under
the banyan tree.
"Thank goodness
for that," said the cat.
"Now what?"
said the crow.
"I'm bored."

"It's time for tea," said the cat. "And we have
some visitors. I shall pour and you may
pass the cakes."